Rhymes of Life

Drizzlery

Ukiyoto Publishing

All global publishing rights are held by

Ukiyoto Publishing

Published in 2024

Content Copyright © Jhowel Rhane M. Balilahon (Drizzlery)

ISBN 9789362694720

*All rights reserved.
No part of this publication may be reproduced,
transmitted, or stored in a retrieval system, in any form
by any means, electronic, mechanical, photocopying,
recording or otherwise, without the prior permission of
the publisher.*

The moral rights of the authors have been asserted.

*This book is sold subject to the condition that it shall not by
way of trade or otherwise, be lent, resold, hired out or
otherwise circulated, without the publisher's prior
consent, in any form of binding or cover other than that in
which it is published.*

www.ukiyoto.com

Contents

The First Man I Love, My First Heartbreak	1
The Depths of Loneliness	5
First Puppy Love	7
Friendly Zone	8
Love is a Poem	9
Her Second Heartbreak	12
About the Author	*14*

(Agony of Eleven)

The First Man I Love, My First Heartbreak

He was the first, her heart's delight,
A beacon shining through the night,
To sweep her off her feet so free,
A life with love, pure ecstasy.

On dates they ventured, hand in hand,
Exploring dreams in a wonderland,
His eyes ignited sparks within,
A tale of love about to begin.

Their laughter echoed, hearts entwined,
A symphony of emotions defined,
With every step, a world anew,
Love's magic painting skies so blue.

He gave her flowers, petals rare,
A fragrant gift beyond compare,
A symbol of a love so true,
A symbol of colors grew.

Sweet and fair, their beauty spoke,
Of feelings deep, like dreams evoked,
She held them close, a treasure rare,
A symbol of a love to wear.

In her heart, a spark did gleam,
A fairy tale, a cherished dream,
She felt like royalty, a queen,
In his arm, a radiant scene.

The joy because of the blossoming young girl's first love. That "he" referred to the person she falls for, the one who becomes a pivotal figure in her journey of emotions. Their interactions are filled with innocence and excitement as they go on dates, their connection deepening with each passing moment. The imagery of his hand in hers symbolizes the tender connection they share, while the description of a world aglow signifies the euphoria and enchantment that come with the early stages of love.

But hidden shadows slowly grew,
A tons of secrets, known to few,
A tale unraveling, untrue,
A love once pure, now lost in blue.

Drizzlery

In her heartbreak's bitter sting,
The echoes of deceit took wing,
A story tainted, torn apart,
A shattered trust, a wounded heart.

The love she thought was pure and grand,
A castle built on shifting sand,
Illusions spun with care and grace,
Now crumbled in a dark embrace.

Falsehood's whispers veiled the truth,
Deceitful steps in love's sweet youth,
Her little heart, once full of glee,
Now torn apart, so painfully.

And as the poem turns its gaze,
Through wistful haze, a hidden phase,
The revelation swift imparts,
A truth that strikes like piercing darts.

The man that she first loved so true,
Set standards high, skies clear and blue.
A model for the love she'd seek,
In every future journey's peak.

A twist of fate, a painful start,
A bond once strong, now torn apart,

In shadows cast, emotions smart,
It's her own father who broke her heart.

With a heavy weight on her chest, the revelation unfolds like a cruel riddle,
that she prays will never be solved....
Now she wonders,
"How many hearts have been broken because of the painful reality caused by their own first love, which is their father?"

(Darkest Twelve)

The Depths of Loneliness

In every deed I've done, in every place I roam,
All I sense is the weight of mine, a burden to everyone.
I sense your remorse, tied to moments with me,
Apologies for adding to your darkness, it's my plea.

Will the world unravel
her struggle to endure the self-worn play?
In the ink of scars she carries,
penned by the disappointments that linger and stay.

Shall they see her justified,
a victim in the drama of pain's endless ride?
Or shall they accuse, apprehend,
branding her the sculptor of her suffering's bitter blend?

The moon turns red, like my thoughts in my head,
Is it carrying a weight, just like I do in bed?

The sky is dark, like the shadows in my eye,
Does it also feel scared, like I sometimes pry?

The moon's red glow, like my feelings unsaid,
Isn't it bleeding, too, just like me in my bed?

(Puppy Love Thirteen)

First Puppy Love

There's a lot of humans in the world

But there is nothing like you

And, that is the thing

That makes you special—

I like you.

(Bitter Fourteen)

Friendly Zone

I want to shout, I long to say,
"I love you," in every way.
Those three words trapped in my chest,

When and how shall I tell you?
If she's your Juliet, you're my Romeo,

"I love you," you said, but not for me,
For her, your love flows endlessly.
She's the victor in your love's game,
While I, the silent loser, remain.

(Lovely Fifteen)

Love is a Poem

:: As the end draws near, our destinies intertwine, stay with me, by my side, till the final moment we ride. If our love now wanes and sorrow drips like rain, let us endure and suffer through love's rough weather.

:: As the embers of hope flicker and die, in your arms; I will bid goodbye, with every fleeting breath, we journey towards our inevitable death. Let us cling to each moment, cherishing what's left till the final beat of our hearts, till the final breath of our souls, till the curtain falls on this tragic tale we've been cast.

I'll watch you from afar
Just like how I watch
the night sky full of stars.

I'll admire you secretly

Just like how I admire
the moon silently.

I'll wait you
Just like how I
Wait for the sunset

I'll love you privately
Just like how I
Love the astronomy.

Because, My Love
you're my own
definition of galaxy.
In the middle of the night, where everyone's asleep
He can hear the two people's hearts, with a love on its beat.
Using his bow with an arrow in it
He pulled the string of the instrument of love, and released it as the time tick.

We going to tackle a story of winged cherub.
He, who's active 24/7 for its hope
Because love dont sleep, it just went deep
And the harder he pulled the string, the deeper it will hit.

Drizzlery

In the middle of the night, where everyone's asleep
The matchmaker of love, he's wide-awake
Hunting its prey who's willing to take the risk
Its his full-time responsibility, at least.

In the middle of the night, where everything's cold
The legend of love, it won't get old.
He, a roman god of love, a story to be told
About the cupid and a string, any heart can be hold.

(Not so Sweet Sixteen)

Her Second Heartbreak

While I was but a chapter in his book, you see,
Her title, her journey, will forever be free.
Through the pages, my story was unfurled,
Yet she, the embodiment of a world.

While I was only a chapter in his book, you see,
She is the title, the one who sets hearts free.
But in the pages turned and the stories untold,
My chapter's essence shall forever unfold.

The shadow of the past, how do they last?
Luminescence of moments that went too fast.
They stuck in our minds, both good and bad,
Reminding us of the memories we've had.

But memories aren't always sweet,
Sometimes they're bitter, sometimes they're bleak.
The pain of something that we can't forget,
Or the regret of a mistake we can't correct.

Shadow of the past, a double-edged sword,

They bring us comfort, yet leave us floored.
For even though they're a part of who we are,
They can leave us with emotional scars.

But still, we hold on to these memories,
For they make up the fabric of our histories.
It will appear behind us, when we least expect,
A silent reminder, that we can't forget.

Yet, in the midst of darkness, there is still light,
A chance for redemption, a chance to make things right.
And yes, scars fade as time goes by,
But it will remain till the day I die.

About the Author

Drizzlery, who prefers to be called Rhane, is a graduating student with a fondness for cats and dogs. At 17 years old, she is on the brink of turning 18. Rhane has a deep passion for reading, which sparked her interest in writing poetry from a young age. Throughout the pandemic, she sought solace in stories during times of loneliness. Faced with a desire to express her thoughts but lacking an audience, Rhane turned to writing. The sensation of being heard through her poems sends shivers down her spine. Since then, she has harbored dreams of becoming a writer and poetess. Rhane holds the position of eldest daughter in her family.